I0538256

BÊTE NOIRE
FEAR IS JUST A POINT OF VIEW

Editors:

A. W. Gifford

Jennifer L. Gifford

www.betenoiremagazine.com

Bête Noire is published by Dark Opus Press a division of Charm Noir
Omnimedia

ISBN-13: 978-0-9985931-2-8
ISBN-10: 0-9985931-2-5

In This Issue

Self Defense

Megan E. Cassidy

This whole thing is nonsense. You know it was the girl's own fault. I guarantee it. But if I must answer your questions, I must. For the record, my name is Nora VanHousen. At the time of the incident, I was standing just over there by the kitchen island. Beatrice and I had been counting the oyster forks and were about to move onto my grandmother's pearl-handled caviar spoons when we heard a commotion in the foyer. I assumed someone was here to see Parker. Well, of course, I called for Louisa right away. I was not about to rush out into my entryway without having our caller properly announced. I had no way of knowing that there was no caller and the tumult was caused by Louisa herself. It didn't even occur to me until Beatrice said, "Mummy, I do believe that our Louisa is screaming in the foyer."

Of course, those weren't her exact words. She is only four years old, you know. Still the sentiment was the same, and Beatrice is quite articulate for someone her age. Our little ritual of counting the silver has helped to develop her mathematical skills as well. She's a shoo-in for Berkshire Prep next fall. Verbal fluency and math are only part of her education, of course. She is already taking art and music lessons as well. Beyond that, it is my duty as her mother to teach her how to be a lady. Keeping track of the servants is such trying work, and I've been very careful to teach my daughter all the tricks my mother taught me.

Mother would begin in the dining hall. We had large Persian rugs in that room. They were terribly heavy and difficult to clean. Sometimes, the help would simply lift the corners to dust under them or run a vacuum over the top. This may be the way some people clean their carpets, but to do it properly, you have to pick them up, take them outside, and beat the dust out of them at least once a month. Rolling them up to clean underneath is required weekly. Maids can be so lazy, you know.

Forgive my rudeness. You probably don't know. Well, let me tell you, they are horribly indolent if you don't keep them in line. Mother and I would go to each rug in the dining hall, and then move to those in the parlor, the music room, and the gallery. She would hold up one end of the rug and I'd crawl underneath and leave loose change in the middle. Sometimes merely a quarter or dime, but other times, we'd leave silver dollars and paper money as well.

We had to test their honesty, of course. If the money was still there the next week, the maid was slovenly and had not cleaned things thoroughly. If the money was gone, she was a liar and a thief. Some-one who takes a quarter will just as easily steal a diamond pendant or a husband, if given the chance. If the coins and money were stacked neatly on the nearest table or handed directly to mother, the maid passed her first examination.

This was my favorite little trick as a child, and has proven to be quite useful now I'm running a household myself. There were other tests, of course. Counting the silver each week to make sure none was missing through either thievery or carelessness. Going through the servant quarters to inspect for neatness. Speaking a false rumor in a girl's presence and waiting to see whether it would return to us through the usual channels. I don't know what I would have done without Mother's guidance. However, would I know whom to keep on and whom to dismiss?

What in the world is that racket? How long are you people going to be tramping through my house? I'll have to replace every carpet in this place. And now, you're getting black dust all over my draperies. Get your filthy paws off of my curtains!

I certainly will not answer your questions. Not until you tell your men to get away from my windows. Those are velvet drapes. The stains will never come out. The girl didn't even die in that room. She died in the foyer, for goodness sakes. I will send you the bill, believe you me. Those curtains cost over a thousand a panel.

That's better. Now, to return to the matter at hand, Louisa's perfor-mance was far below par. Over the past few years, I eliminated Kathe-rine, Angela, and Therese from our employ after they failed the coin test I described to you. Pamela was next. She was dismissed after only three months because she did slip-shod disorganized work. The girl forgot to fetch my dry cleaning three times in succession and left spots on the silver. Then I found a dust bunny under my daughter's bed, which was the last straw. I will not expose my Beatrice to such inhumane living conditions.

After Pamela came Darcy. She was simply marvelous. Ran our household like a Navy submarine. All affairs in order. All details attended to. I never had to lift a finger. I should ring her as soon as possible. Forgive me, but I'm afraid we must conclude our discussion. If I don't call her now, I'll forget.

Why shouldn't I leave? Haven't I answered your questions already? I might remind you that I have a team of lawyers on retainer. They might specialize in real estate, but I'm sure they could find friends who are expert in criminal matters. If you'd like me to keep talking, you'd better watch your manners, young man. I've been very cooperative so far, but I might find a reason to leave if you speak to me that way again.

Thank you. Parker, would you be a dear and have Oliver ring Darcy and offer her Louisa's former position? I've never attempted to rehire anyone, and today has been such a strain.

Oliver is Parker's secretary. He runs a ship almost as tight as Darcy's. I do believe he missed her a bit when she left. He'll be ever so grateful we're bringing her back on.

Do I think that he was involved with Louisa's death? Don't be ridiculous. I told you that the girl did this to herself. That's the only explanation for it.

No. I shouldn't think that Darcy knows Louisa either. They have quite different backgrounds, you know, regardless of their positions in this household. And I can't see why she'd have a grudge against me. I did have to let her go, but she seemed quite civil about it.

Typically, our cook Anna prepares all our meals, but we had an impromptu dinner party one night when Anna had her day out. Darcy agreed to cater the party for us in her stead. The meal was delightful, but unfortunately, she served individual chocolate soufflés for dessert. They deflated like old withered balloons, collapsing in on themselves, one after another. It was quite an embarrassment. I wanted to forgive the poor girl for it, but Parker's mother attended the supper and she insisted that Darcy leave. She was appalled. Said we would be the laughingstock of the entire town if we didn't let her go. I could see that she was quite correct, though once Louisa came to us, I immediately regretted the decision.

She understood my dilemma, as any proper housekeeper would. If she agrees to return, I may just give her that promotion. Louisa was a nightmare in comparison. She was completely incompetent. She couldn't set the table correctly, even after I showed her where to place everything. The cake forks and dessert spoons were never in their proper places, and the cocktail forks were simply slapped down next to the salad forks instead of laid properly across the soup spoons.

I wanted to dismiss her straight away, but Parker said that she should stay on. He said, "Nora. You know that proper training takes more than just three weeks. Give the girl a little more time."

I don't like your tone. What precisely do you mean, "Had Mr. VanHousen taken an interest in any of your other employees?" What are you implying?

If you're asking whether Parker was having a dalliance with the girl, the idea is laughable. Of course he wasn't. You've examined the body. Louisa was absolutely enormous. That was my primary objection to her presence in my home.

No, I do not care how much my servants weigh, Officer Henry. As long as they perform to my standards, they can weigh whatever they choose. I objected to the fact that she was secretly eating us out of house and home.

How long is this going to continue? The Junior League is sponsoring a hospital benefit this evening, and it will take simply ages for me to prepare.

Fine. Fine. A few more minutes then. At any rate, Louisa was secretly eating my food. It was revolting how many items she'd pinched from the icebox. I had no proof of it, but Anna our cook mentioned to me that things seemed to go missing from the pantry and the icebox. A tin of cookies here, a slice of cake there. At first, I thought that perhaps my dear little Beatrice was indulging in a sweet-tooth I knew nothing about. When I confronted her about it, she cried and said, "Mummy, everyone at school is allowed cookies. May I try one someday?"

I replied, "Of course not. How will you ever keep your girlish figure if you start gobbling down treats every chance you have? Don't you want to look pretty for your debutante ball?" She demurred to my wisdom.

I then asked my husband, but Parker is on a strict regimen that he adheres to with the discipline of a samurai. He allows himself one sweet every other week. I, myself rarely partake; I'm Banting, you know. Unless I was secretly a somnambulist, Louisa was certainly the culprit. But I couldn't prove it, you see. My mother had never taught me how to approach this particular problem. Money, yes. Husbands, of course, but preventing that lies mainly in the hiring. Men are lustful and can be turned by nearly anyone who winks at them, but an older dowdy woman like Darcy or a slovenly girl like Louisa would hardly catch Parker's eye.

I have never before had anyone invade my home in such a manner. The food came first. Money would be next. Then who knows? My friend Ingrid Sissle once had a maid who conspired with a gang of robbers. She let them into the home while Ingrid was summering in the Riviera, and they cleared out everything. They even took the crystals right off the chandeliers. Well, of course, they tracked down the culprits, and most of her things were returned, but they were never in the same condition. She was forced to buy eleven new chandeliers. It was a travesty and Ingrid nearly had a nervous breakdown because of it. She left for Aspen and was unable to return for three whole months.

Was I concerned Louisa Washington might attack my home? Haven't you been listening to a word I've said? She already had on more than one occasion. She entered my pantry and my icebox and stole from me. Louisa was a liar and a thief and she had to leave. How could I allow such a moral degenerate to remain in my household?

I laid a trap for her, and she took the bait. It worked better than I ever could have dreamed. I'm going to keep it in my list of monthly examinations, to prevent such blatant disregard for my safety from ever occurring again.

I bought fifty petit fours from that delightful little Parisian bakery around the corner. Then, I sent Louisa out for the afternoon. She was so delighted, she never even questioned my motives. Once she was gone, I went outside and enlisted the help of our gardener Tony. He picked a basket full of azalea blossoms and brought them into the house.

Once they were washed, I instructed our cook Anna to sugar the blossoms and I used them to top each one of the tiny cakes. We counted the petit fours again before putting them into the pantry. When Louisa returned, I said, "Louisa, there are petit fours left over from this afternoon's tea. We may have to throw them all away, but be careful not to touch them for now. Ingrid might be coming over to call this afternoon." She agreed and that I repeated the warning last night.

This morning, I discovered the untrustworthy gluttonous girl didn't just limit herself to one. In fact, she ate six, the greedy little thing. She probably believed I would not notice! Well, of course after consuming the delightful delicacies, she became ill. Who wouldn't after having all that sugar?

Of course, I never imagined she'd start choking the way she did. The book I found in Parker's library stated that in an adult, particularly a larger one, the flowers would only induce a bit of light vomiting, and possibly some dizziness. Then again, the girl did ingest six times the amount I intended her to, so again, her gluttony did her in.

What are you doing? Why are you grabbing my arm? You're hurting me!

Taking me in for further questioning? You can't do this to me. I didn't force feed her anything. I specifically told the idiot girl *not* to eat the cakes. I warned her twice, and she did it anyway. If Parker had shot a burglar breaking into Beatrice's room, would you arrest him? Of course not. It comes to the same thing. She was stealing from us. What other choice did I have?

Get these handcuffs off of me at once! Don't you know who I am? Louisa was invading my home like a rat in a barn, devouring every scrap of cornmeal or spare egg it can find. I was saving my home from a thief. I haven't done anything wrong. It was self-defense.

Megan Cassidy *is an English professor and the author of books for middle grade, young adult, and adult readers.*

Coming out this June, Megan's second book, The Misadventures of Marvin Miller, *is a middle grade novel recounting one boy's hilarious summer as he tries to impress the girl he likes. Megan's first novel,* Always, Jessie *is a YA novel charting one girl's recovery from an eating disorder and exercise addiction in a diverse recovery community. She also writes for adults under the name M.C. Hall.* Smothered, *Megan's adult epistolary mystery, will be published in the Fall of 2017.*

Megan's other work has been featured in Silver Blade Magazine, Pilcrow & Dagger, Bette Noire, Fiction on the Web, Flash Fiction Press, Dying Dahlia Review, Citron Review, and the Centum Press One Hundred Voices Anthology.

Exit

Bob Johnston

The months and years pass by,
The falling leaves and fading light
Mark the beginning of the end.
In springtime long ago I was immortal
And unafraid, the master of my soul.
But now the dark descends.

Where have the dreams all gone?
The visions of a better world?
The joy of living in the sun?
All faded, withered, fallen like the leaves
That wait for winter snow to give them peace.

Springtime will never come again,
And darkness will be eternal.

Bob Johnston *is a retired petroleum engineer, translator of Russian literature, and an ex-drunk. He started to write serious poetry at age sixty; and now, more than three decades later, he is still trying to catch up. His poems have appeared in twenty-odd journals and in a collection of his poetry titled* At the Rim *(Sunstone Press, 2011). His poems reflect a dim view of the universe and outrage at having been propelled into a century he will never understand.*

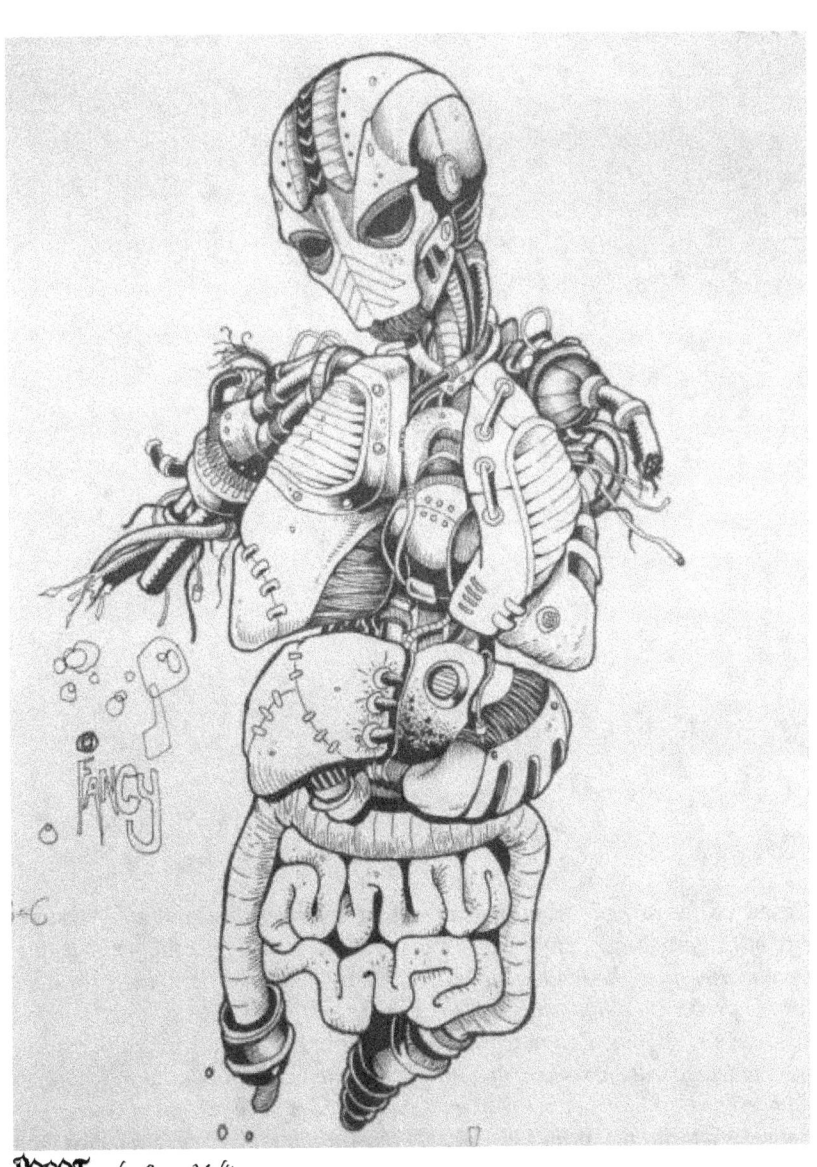

ROBOT   by Cesar Valtierra

Cesar Valtierra *hails from the sun soaked desert of the wild, wild western city of El Paso, Texas. He wields a pencil like an outlaw gunslinger, drawing up a storm since the tender age of two. He is infamous throughout the land for his provocative ink drawings, his meticulous vector illustrations, and his eye catching graphic design work. Like a thief in the night, Mr. Valtierra is a man of few words but one who with his work makes quite an impression. He follows the beat of his own drum and answers to no one; except of course, his fiancée Victoria, the love of his life, his inspiration and muse. And their two cats, Chubs and Pretty Boy.*

If you think you can handle the awesomeness, feel free to check out his work at www.cesarvaltierra.com and of course his comic book featuring the adventures of Balazo, the pint-sized detective at www.tonybalazo.com.

Pie in the Sky

Brian Koukol

As a clown in your prime, backwards pants and embarrassing falls can rake in the laughs. But then you get old and do the same stuff on accident. And that's just sad. When Bozo falls, it's a rollicking good time. When grandpa falls, it's time for a hip replacement and pneumonia and a tacky urn on an MDF mantel somewhere.

That's what happened to Dennis in ten. He slipped on a banana peel in the dayroom three weeks ago and died. He was my friend.

Since then, two more residents had followed, one each week. Otto in room nine and Deirdre in eight. You can see the pattern.

I was in room seven.

Today was my day, it seemed. But if I was going out, I was going out in clown white, dignity intact.

I pulled the dusty shoebox from my closet with a foot and kicked it over to the chair in front of the mirror. Inside the box was a black eyeliner pencil. I sat down with it, determined to replicate the tight lines of my heyday. But my tremors wouldn't cooperate.

Back before I got Parkinson's, I was a mime. A classic Pierrot with moves of wind and water. But I lost my grace with my fine motor skills and found myself playing the tramp. Then the auguste. The butt of the joke.

We're all augustes here. Even out of costume. Though I might not have to worry about it much longer.

I threw the pencil across the room in disgust and wiped the sloppy mess from my face. Out came the Mehron black. I dug in with an inelegant finger and smeared shaky rings around my eyes and lips, transforming myself like some valiant Lakota pledged to battle. Then, the white. I submerged myself in its reassuring aroma as I applied it, riding the carousel backwards on a catalyst of scent memory and rote. For an instant, I was young again. I was whole again. Then I glanced at the mirror.

The defeated mug that looked back was more demon than Deburau. It was me, but a weathered, wrinkled me. An overbaked cake, smothered in icing to hide its dry, hard truth.

With a sigh, I slipped into my ample white robes and stuffed my head into a black skullcap. A quick glance through my cracked door revealed an empty corridor. It was time.

I passed Deirdre's door first. A handful of narrow, uninflated balloons hung from it, stapled together in the rough shape of a stick figure horse. She had been an accomplished balloon twister until rheumatoid arthritis had ruined her. Now she was dead, strangled by a braided strap of her chosen medium.

Otto's room was next. His orthopedic shoes were still outside his door. He'd tried to paint them into novelty with sparkling nail polish lifted from visiting relations, but most of it had flaked off. Now they were only an anecdote in a life defined by its end—aspiration of a cream pie.

A narrow strip of sunlight shone through the door opposite, but it slammed shut when I looked over. Just some spectator waiting for the blow-off.

Up ahead, beyond Dennis's room, was the corner leading to the dining hall. I hesitated in front of it, unsure of what would be waiting for me behind. An oversized hammer in the face? Garrotting by tightrope?

I took a deep breath and shuffled around the corner.

Deserted.

The emptiness continued into the dining hall. Even the tables were put away. All but one, that is.

Wrapped in blue gingham oilcloth and topped with an ostentatious cupcake, it sat just inside the open supply closet. A trap, obviously, but I found I didn't care. In fact, the discovery came as a relief. And why not? What did I have to live for?

That's the thing about clowns. About why we do what we do. Forget all that nonsense about making kids laugh and bringing joy to the world. We're trying to fill a hole, just like everybody else. Only difference is we do it through self-deprecation and the adulation of the crowd. And when you lose the crowd, what's left?

I picked up the cupcake.

Three sharp notes issued from a hidden calliope and the floor dropped out from under my feet, plunging me into darkness. The fall was short, but hard, and my hip took the brunt of it. I lay on my back for a few minutes, groaning and dreading the worst. Finally, I gathered my courage and flexed the joint.

Sweet relief. It wasn't broken. I was going to be okay, at least for the time being.

Before my eyes had gotten used to the darkness, a spotlight snapped on and I found myself alone on a makeshift stage. As I struggled to rise to my feet, I bumped my head on a low ceiling, but, when I looked up, there was nothing there. I dropped onto all fours and tried to crawl from the stage, but again my head hit an unseen barrier. I threw my hands out and they too were stopped, my fingertips spreading against an invisible wall. And then it dawned on me. I was trapped in a glass box.

As I sat on stage, a mime locked in a cliché, my heart contorted in my chest. This was my fate. My banana peel. My balloon animal noose.

I kicked at my transparent cage. Punched it. Threw my shoulders against it. Fought it until I lay in a heap, panting and exhausted.

A great roar of applause erupted from the darkness. The house lights came up, revealing a full gallery of excited families. Only they weren't real families, but cardboard approximations. Their cheers, playback from some better time.

It was glorious.

That's the magic of illusion. Lies become truth with the help of a willing participant. And I found myself more than willing.

Brian Koukol *lives on the Central Coast of California, where he somehow finds time to write between soaking up rays and eating his weight in avocados. This story, like all of his fiction, is written with voice recognition software on account of his lifelong nemesis, muscular dystrophy.*
Visit his author website: http://www.briankoukol.com/

Daily Dose of Vitamin EVP

Ash Krafton

Don't play back the answering machine
I told you we needed to upgrade
one of those in-line services
that doesn't need any machinery
so much easier to access remotely

(probably throws off harmful EMF too)

But no, you said, you like the old one
that clunk of electronics that sits on the kitchen table
blinking its hello when you get home
the delete button that sometimes sticks
making for awkward message mismanagement

Well, something else likes it, too
I can't tell if it's man or woman
or a terrified, screaming child/animal?
but lately there's been weird messages
even when the caller id said no calls came through

(turns out I was wrong about the remote access)

And the messages won't delete, they
just keep showing up, like history echoes
sometimes the lights flicker
or I hear footsteps in the crawlspace
and then the blinking number 1

I can't play them anymore
the pounding of blood in my ears
the dial tone I hear buzzing in the cellar
those slithery whispers won't ever say goodbye
time we lost that landline

(our health might depend upon it)

Pushcart Prize nominee Ash Krafton's *work has appeared in several journal,
including* Polu Texni, Big Pulp, Silver Blade, *and* Bete Noire. *She's also
the author of novel-length fiction, such as the* Demimonde trilogy *as well as*
The Heartbeat Thief *(under the pen name* AJ Krafton). *She's a member of
SFPA and resides in the heart of the Pennsylvania coal region with her family
and bossy German Shepherd dog.*

The Thing in the Field

Lawrence Buentello

Settled between two low hills, the field spread out from the road a hundred yards from east to west, and a hundred feet north to where it met a dry ravine that served as a terminus for the mesquite and juniper trees. Jordan had last seen it as a child, but even now the same sensation crept over his skin, as if something invisible were welcoming him with its touch. The grass, green and yellow under the early summer sun, danced delicately in the warm breeze. He wondered why no one had developed the land – the city had grown exponentially in the last forty years, extending in all directions, housing developments, strip malls, office buildings – but not this part of the city.

He felt a wave of *deja vu* turning back time to when the field was truly isolated, and smelled of heat and dust; when shadows moved through the undulating grasses, beckoning. Only remnants of a foundation remained of the house where his family had lived forty years ago. The house where Wayne's family had lived still stood down the street, but was now boarded up and abandoned. Perhaps Wayne's mother and father had filled it with so much grief that no one else had wanted to live in it.

There was a time, though, when a family lived in each house, and two boys living near each other became friends. There was a time, a very brief time, when Jordan knew adventure in his life, and a ticking sense of excitement in his heart. Then Wayne disappeared, and life transformed into something dull and oppressive.

Jordan gazed over the field another few minutes before limping painfully toward the rental car he'd parked off the road. His left knee had begun giving him grief during the drive, as it always did after sitting too long.

He'd flown into the city for his father's funeral. Otherwise, he would still be in Dallas brooding over the papers his lawyer had given him. Divorce, aside from the emotional turmoil it produced, created nothing but a series of decisions to be considered, concessions to be made. His father's death had interrupted his excursion into self-pity quite effectively. The man's passing was no surprise — he'd previously survived two heart surgeries — but Jordan's mother's sorrow and her own emotional withdrawal from the proceedings filled his hours with much more than just an abiding sense of loss. He felt utterly hopeless, as if nothing remaining of his life was worth salvaging.

Only the field remained, seemingly untouched by the years.

He hadn't planned to drive across the city to see the houses and the field, but his father was now interred, all salutations were concluded, and his mother refused to comment on the proceedings. She wasn't an uncaring woman — but she'd always been distant, emotionally unavailable, perhaps because of the effects of early poverty and the loss of youthful dreams. He'd be in the city for another couple of days, until his return flight brought him back to Dallas and the details of his divorce from Sherry. Time he'd allotted to console his mother. But if his mother wanted to remain uncommunicative, why not visit old haunts?

What a pathetic life, he thought as he slid into the driver's seat, pulling at his left leg awkwardly. *What a damned, meaningless life.*

At some point in everyone's life, at least in Jordan's philosophy, the good fight had to be declared a victory or a defeat. Some people's lives were simply failures, and no amount of positive thinking would ever change the outcome.

He drove away from the field, believing he would never return.

The next morning, Jordan woke from a dream of walking through the field.

For a moment, he didn't remember where he was, or how he'd gotten there — he sat up in bed and stared at the pictures on the wall, which were not his, until he remembered the funeral. He lay back down, inhaling deeply. The bedroom, which had once been his, had been converted into a guestroom for guests his parents seldom entertained. A bookshelf filled with paperbacks, magazines, and toys had been his only defense against the world. Now nothing of his childhood remained.

He glanced at his wristwatch and thought the sun would be rising soon. He certainly couldn't sleep any longer, so he dressed and sat at the table in the kitchen, thinking about brewing coffee, but only staring at his hands on the table. His mother was still sleeping.

The dream lay tenuously in his memory, brief flashes of faces, images half-real and half-fantasy. Wayne appeared in the dream, still ten years old, smiling, his face drawn, not quite ugly, but set with mismatched features that were nearly ugly. Skinny as a rail, he waved his arm at Jordan to hurry up, and Jordan, laughing in the dream, pulled at his pants leg in a pathetic attempt to move his crippled leg a little faster. At first, the feeling was exhilarating, as if they were searching for hidden treasure. But as his friend ran farther ahead a feeling of dread overcame Jordan, growing as the distance between them grew. When Wayne was finally out of sight in the tall grass, and Jordan slowed, and finally stopped because he didn't know which way to run, he felt afraid. The shadows grew longer before him, the wind intensified. He heard a faint voice calling out, though he didn't know if it belonged to Wayne. When he felt so full of dread that he thought he would cry, he heard a terrible scream, a sound Jordan had never heard in life —

Jordan gazed up from his hands when his mother finally entered the kitchen. He said nothing, and she said nothing as she filled the coffee maker with water and turned on the machine.

His mother had an old face, older than her years. She seemed terribly decrepit, lost in sagging skin and wrinkles. Wrapped in her robe, she could have been an Egyptian artifact. They sat in silence until the coffee was brewed, and then they sat at the table silently drinking coffee. Neither wished to talk about his pending divorce, or his father's death, or anything relevant to life.

He finally said, "Do you remember the Sewell family?"

His mother stared at him curiously for a moment before replying. "Yes," she said, in a voice strained by days of crying. "We used to live near them. A long time ago."

"Forty years." He nodded, but had difficulty finding anything coherent to say. The dream confused him, though he knew he wanted to talk about Wayne. "Do you remember their son?"

His mother blinked, and he could sense her confusion. "Yes, of course. That was an awful business."

"I drove by our old place on the Southside yesterday."

"I haven't been to that part of the city since we left."

"It hasn't changed." He sipped his coffee, then said, "That old rental of ours is long gone, though."

"It was a terrible place," his mother said, "always too cold in winter, always too hot in summer. Why do you mention it?"

"I don't know."

"Why did you want to see it?"

"I don't know that, either."

"It was a horrible business, that kidnapping. They never found him, you know."

"I know."

"That's why we moved. Your father wouldn't put you in that kind of danger. It was so difficult finding a new place to live. We had no money."

"Yes, I remember."

"But it led to better things."

Jordan didn't know what to say. Better things? Economically, at least. His father found increasingly better jobs, assisted by training programs created for impoverished, undereducated people, the type of welfare Jordan knew intimately in his youth. After living in several apartments, they actually moved into their own house. Jordan finished his education, and eventually his father retired, having hammered out a meaningful existence from his circumstances. But Jordan's mother was now seventy-two, and alone, and he wondered what would happen when she became too feeble to care for herself. Perhaps that was his next trial in life, becoming a caretaker for an elderly parent. But without a wife or family of his own, and being middle-aged and partially crippled, exactly what would he be sacrificing?

"Life was so different then," his mother said, leaning back in her chair. "We had no computers, no cell phones, no complications. People were much more isolated. Relationships meant more, you actually talked to people, did things other than watch television. The world is so different now."

"Do you miss the old days?" he asked.

His mother shook her head. "Not in the least. We were so poor in the old days. I hated that part of life. But things got better."

There was something in the field, he thought to himself, *Wayne said*

he'd seen it, hiding in the grass —

"Why did you ask about the Sewell boy?" his mother said.

They said he was kidnapped, but I know he wasn't — it was the thing in the field —

"No reason," he said. "He just came to mind."

"He was a weird little boy."

"He may have been weird, but he was the only boy in the neighborhood that wanted to be friends with a gimp."

"Don't talk about yourself that way. Don't!"

He sighed, hating the feelings that were boiling inside his gut like a slow poison. "I know, I know. But it's true."

"You've lived a good life."

He had nothing more to say on the subject. "We should go through the insurance papers."

"There's still time for that," his mother said softly, and then retreated into silence.

In Texas in the 1970s, a boy only had a finite number of options for entertainment. Reading — comic books, in particular — watching the three or four available television channels, though limited by what his parents were watching or by what they allowed him to watch, and playing outside, with plastic soldiers, cars, or other toys if he had toys at all, or just sticks and rocks if he didn't.

Jordan remembered Wayne Sewell as a master of their limited environment, shaping imaginary worlds that he and Jordan could explore without the need for money or toys. Both boys came from poor families, but being poor could only delay a boy's enjoyment, not kill it outright.

Jordan and Wayne spent endless summer days sitting on the porch steps of either's house, first Wayne reading a story aloud about flying saucers, then Jordan reciting a 'true' account of tracking the Yeti in the Himalayas. Together, they talked endlessly about the Apollo moon missions, the nature of the solar system, and the exploits of their favorite super heroes, pacing up and down the road between their houses, Wayne waving his skinny arms excitedly and Jordan limping slowly beside him.

They also played in the huge field between the hills, searched for toads in the ravine, and hid from the sun beneath the mesquite trees during the hottest part of the day.

For two boys who were the target of endless derision from other children, a summer away from school, from taunting voices, was a joy. Jordan would never make fun of Wayne's facial features or spindly physique, and Wayne would never belittle Jordan because of his malformed leg. Together, away from everyone else, they were just two normal boys. That summer was the only time Jordan felt whole, felt as if he really belonged in the world.

Wayne's imagination was more developed than Jordan's. He would conjure incredible stories of past exploits, of actually *seeing* flying saucers, of experiencing things Jordan knew his friend could never have experienced. Jordan never reproached his friend over these exaggerations; they were part of the game, part of their escape from a difficult life.

Neither the heat nor the swarming mosquitoes could detract from the joy they experienced that summer.

But the summer ended the night Wayne vanished.

Jordan had talked to the police, of course, and told them about the field, but they didn't understand. They thought he meant to say that there was someone in the field, hiding there perhaps, or living in the trees by the ravine. But that's not what he meant. He never told them that he was with Wayne the night the boy disappeared. He was afraid to tell them—he was afraid they might think he had something to do with it—

"There's something in the field," Wayne told him one morning as Jordan closed the door to his house and limped down the steps of the porch.

Jordan, who had been concentrating on buttoning his shirt, didn't understand. "What's in the field?"

Wayne stood with the sun at his back, a thin silhouette with a shadowy face. For a moment, he seemed inhuman. "I don't know."

Jordan stared up from his shirt buttons. "Then how do you know something's there?"

"I was over there this morning," Wayne said, sitting on the porch steps. "I was cutting across the field to get to the ravine. About halfway through the grass I felt funny, like I was being watched. I looked around a while, but I couldn't see anything. I don't know, I just *felt* like something was in the grass watching me."

Jordan sat next to his friend, his joy of the morning slowly being replaced by a slight sensation of fear. But since Wayne was an excellent storyteller, this was probably just his latest wild invention. He smiled and nodded, playing along.

Wayne continued, his thin face serious. Jordan had trouble seeing the lie in it. "I thought someone might be hiding in the grass, but I couldn't see anyone. Then I thought it must be a dog or a cat, or maybe a bird, but I couldn't see anything. It was like it was invisible."

"Invisible?"

"Like it wasn't from this world."

Jordan laughed then, certain it was a joke. How Wayne kept such a straight face he didn't know. "You're just making it up."

"I'm *not* making it up. There's something in the field, something no one can see, or, at least, it's hiding so good no one can see it. I *swear* I'm not lying."

Jordan stared into Wayne's eyes, but his friend never betrayed the joke. His fear returned then, like a hand walking up his spine.

"Let's go find it," Wayne said, slapping Jordan on the leg and rising. "Right now, let's go see what it is!"

Jordan stood uncertainly. "What if there really is something there? What if it's *bad*, Wayne?"

"It's not bad, I promise."

"How do you know? If you couldn't see it, how do you know it's not a bad thing?"

Wayne shook his head, as if he were the guardian of some secret knowledge. "I just know. Come on!"

They went, Wayne hurrying down the road excitedly, Jordan following less enthusiastically. They waded into the tall green grass like explorers in an Amazon jungle, sweeping aside the billowing blades in search of something hidden. They moved up and down between the hills, searching, but finding nothing. After a while, Jordan's fear diminished, and then left him altogether. Wayne was obviously mistaken, or had run out of ways to keep his story viable.

They sat under the mesquite trees when the sun began heating up the ground, rolled up their sleeves and pants legs, and threw rocks at the grass.

"There's nothing in the field," Jordan said.

"There *is* something in the field," Wayne said, turning halfway.

"It's there, I know it is. We just can't see it."

Jordan sighed, then picked up another rock, hefting it to see how much effort he'd have to exert in order to hit the nearest tree. "Well, we sure didn't find it, whatever it is."

"It must be something magical. That's why we can't see it. But I *felt* it. I know it's there."

"You're just imagining things."

"No."

They remained silent for a while. Then Wayne said, "I hate it here."

Jordan squinted at his friend through the bright sunlight. "What's wrong with this place?"

"Not *here*, you idiot!" Wayne laughed, waving his thin arms. Jordan laughed, too. Wayne lowered his arms, staring back toward the road. "I hate school, I hate the kids at school. They're always calling me names. I hate my house. It's not even our house. It's too hot. I hate my mother and father."

"You don't hate your mother and father."

Wayne lowered his head. "I don't hate them, I guess. But I don't think they like me any more than the kids at school. They think I'm weird, too. My father never wants to do anything with me."

"My father won't do anything with me, either."

Wayne glanced at Jordan's leg, but only shook his head. "It shouldn't be like this. It should be better."

"How could it be better?"

"I don't know. I just know I don't want to go back to school."

"You *have* to go back to school."

Wayne bit his lip, then said, "I know. I guess I'll just have to keep hating this place until I don't have to be here anymore."

Jordan understood Wayne's feelings. He'd never stated his impressions of school or his family in quite the same way, but he certainly *felt* the same way. It wasn't fair. But at least they could share the summer together. That summer was an emotional oasis in a desert of bad feelings.

Wayne said nothing more of hating the world, or his parents. Instead he said, "I think I know why we can't find it."

"Find what?"

"The thing in the field! It's invisible during the day, so people won't be able to find it. But I'll bet it glows in the dark, like a flying saucer. I'll bet if we came out here tonight we'd see it glowing in the grass."

"My folks won't let me outside after dark."

Wayne stared at Jordan, smiling subtly. "We could sneak out tonight. I'll bring my father's flashlight, the one he used when he was a security guard. We'll come back at night and search the field."

Jordan shook his head, slowly, slowly — he could think of a thousand reasons why it was a terrible idea, the first of which, and the one that promised the most severe consequences, was getting caught.

But Wayne kept talking, and talking persuasively. It was as if he desperately needed to go on this idiotic treasure hunt, and after a while Jordan found himself agreeing, though he was certain they would get caught, and punished badly for it.

That night, after midnight, an hour or so after his parents were in bed, Jordan quietly pushed open the screen on the window of his room and slipped out into the yard. Wayne was waiting for him on the porch steps, a shadowy gargoyle holding a six-cell flashlight. After a whispered plea for Wayne to forget this ridiculous nocturnal adventure, Jordan followed his friend down the street, their footsteps eerily loud in the silence of the night. A gibbous moon hung low on the horizon, casting a frosty light on the slowly moving grass.

They stood on the edge of the road staring over the field. Beyond the grass, the ravine was a backdrop of twisted black shapes.

"I *feel* it," Wayne whispered. "I know it's there. And when we find it, you'll see. It's going to be incredible."

Wayne switched on the flashlight. The beam fell on the field like a white scythe. Then he stepped into the grass. Jordan stayed by the road, his arms crossed, feeling chilled despite the heat. With his friend quickly disappearing into the field, he swallowed once, fought down his fear, and followed.

He purposely let his limp slow him down. He kept Wayne in sight, afraid to be left alone, but also afraid of being alongside his friend if the boy actually found something. He had a feeling that if they did find the thing in the field it might be dangerous, or even evil.

"I think I see it!" Wayne said, his voice no longer a whisper. "It's over here, Jordan! Come on!"

Jordan heard his friend running through the grass, saw the

flashlight beam jerking up and down in the air, moving farther and farther away. But Jordan froze. He couldn't move. Fear rose up in his belly and made him too sick to run. He watched the flashlight's beam grow fainter, heard Wayne's voice grow fainter, too, and pretty soon only the light of the gibbous moon let him see anything at all.

"It's *here*!" Wayne's voice rang out. "It's here! It's —"

That was the last time Jordan would hear his friend's voice. The flashlight's beam died abruptly; for a moment, all Jordan could hear was the wind combing through the grass. Then the crickets and the toads began singing again.

Jordan felt suddenly afraid for Wayne, and suddenly he wasn't frozen any longer. He rushed forward through the grass, almost blindly, in the direction he thought Wayne had gone. He kept calling Wayne's name, over and over, sweeping his arms through the tall grass, wondering if the boy was playing a joke on him, *praying* it was a joke—but he couldn't find Wayne anywhere.

It *had* to be a joke. His friend had dragged him out into the field and then left him. Wayne was probably back on the road, laughing.

Jordan struggled through the grass, away from the blackness of the ravine toward the road. But when he was standing on the asphalt again, he found himself alone. He wanted to shout out Wayne's name, but someone would hear him, tell his parents. What could he do? God, what if there really was something in the field? And it got Wayne?

Jordan began running down the road, struggling to keep his bad leg from locking and sending him sprawling on the asphalt. He felt like crying, but he didn't cry, afraid of making too loud a noise. He pulled himself up through his bedroom window, latched the screen and fell into bed. He knew he would find Wayne sitting on his porch steps the following morning, wearing a satisfied grin. The next morning, Wayne would laugh at him, then tell him 'no hard feelings'. The next morning—

 Fifty years old and feeling much, much older, Jordan stood quietly by the side of the road, glancing back only once to where he'd parked the rental car. He held a small flashlight in his hand, not quite yet necessary in the twilight. Before him the field stood inoffensively, grass whispering at the insistence of the breeze.

The police had come to his door the day following Wayne's disappearance, speaking first to his mother, and then to him when his mother acknowledged that he and Wayne had been friends. He'd said nothing at first, terrified by the thought of admitting he was with Wayne the previous night. Eventually, he told the policeman that Wayne had talked about the field, had told him he might go searching through it one night. That prompted the police to search the field and the ravine, but they found absolutely nothing, not even the six-cell flashlight. This baffled him — he thought they'd surely find some sign of him, but they didn't. When the police questioned him again, he recounted Wayne's feelings about school, and the neighborhood children. But he just couldn't confess to being with Wayne the night the boy disappeared.

When the police ran out of places to search, they speculated that Wayne might have run away. But everyone whispered about an abduction. The police kept searching, and, for all Jordan knew, kept searching for years. No trace of his friend was ever found.

But Wayne couldn't simply have vanished, could he? Something had happened to him, whether he had run away from the life he hated, or was taken from it by some stranger. Or had it been something else?

Jordan switched on the flashlight as he walked into the grass. The grass had seemed impossibly high forty years ago, but he was much taller now and found his way easily. The light continued to fade in the sky as he swept back and forth through the field, casting his beam into the shadows, hoping to see something he hadn't seen forty years earlier. Thinking that maybe —

After a few minutes. he felt something under his shoe, and bent awkwardly to investigate. He had to pull it from the dirt and roots, but when it was in his hand, and he shone a light on it, he shivered. The flashlight illuminated a piece of metal tubing, corroded and caked with dirt, that might have been the case of an old metal flashlight.

But as he examined the rusty artifact, he realized that it could have come from anything. Surely it was only his imagination trying to recast it into something he'd seen a long time ago.

He stood in the middle of the field trying to remember that night, trying to discern whether it was truly joy he heard in

Wayne's voice. How could his friend be so joyous at finding something so frightening? Unless—

Jordan wanted to cry, but no tears came. He walked back slowly through the grass, his bad leg aching with the effort. He had a long way to go before he got back home; not only to his mother's house, but back to Dallas and the divorce proceedings waiting for him. He should be grateful—Sherry had given him twenty years. There had been some good times, as well as bad times. They had no children, but then, he'd never wanted children.

He walked down the dark, deserted road, limping badly.

But before he got back into the car he turned again and stared over the darkened field, and the black shapes in the ravine beyond. Before Wayne had vanished, the place had been magical, wonderful, beautiful.

You found it, didn't you? You found the thing in the field, and it wasn't evil, it wasn't bad. I thought it was bad, like everything else in the world. That's why I couldn't see it. But it couldn't have been bad, because you took it with you when you left. When you left me behind—

Jordan should have been beside his friend that night—not only because he was Wayne's friend, but because hindsight told him that there was perhaps only one moment in a person's life when the magic was real. Assisted by his friend's belief, he might have been able to see it, too.

He dropped the piece of metal onto the road.

Then he slipped into the driver's seat, pulling his bad leg in after himself, before starting the engine and driving away.

Working in multiple genres, **Lawrence Buentello** *has published over 100 short stories and innumerable poems in journals, magazines, and anthologies, many of which can be found in several volumes of collected fiction and poetry. He is also the author or co-author of several novels.* **Buentello** *lives in his hometown of San Antonio, Texas, with his wife, Susan.*

The Doll Conjouer

Marge Simon

In a distant tower,
a young girls parts the curtains
with an incantation,

a magician's hologram
to a higher plane of existence,
an alien sea with strange birds
stitched into the waves.

On the beach, a wooden box,
its nails undone by the tide.

Curious, she's drawn to know its secrets
as she always is with invocations.

The magic holds.

Within the box lie two small dolls,
delicately formed, with eyes of darkest indigo.

They seem familiar, yet dangerously so,
clinging to her garments like insects,
their strange voices wailing in her ears.

She ends the invocation,
returns to the chambers of her world,
only to find them still with her,

unwelcome playmates,
no longer dolls.

Marge Simon *lives in Ocala, Florida and is married to Bruce Boston. She edits a column for the HWA Newsletter,* "Blood & Spades: Poets of the Dark Side," *and serves as Chair of the Board of Trustees. She won the* Strange Horizons Readers Choice Award, 2010, *the SFPA's* Dwarf Stars Award, 2012, *and the* Elgin Award for best poetry collection, 2015. *She has won the* Bram Stoker Award ® *for Poetry, the* Rhysling Award *and the* Grand Master Award *from the SF Poetry Association, 2015. Marge also has work in the anthology* Scary Out There, *a story and poems in* YOU, HUMAN *and fiction in* Chiral Mad 4, 2017, *Dark Regions Press* www.margesimon.com

The Flowers of Failed Labor

Carl R. Jennings

The soil is what is most important in the growth of the seed. I'm sure that there are those that might be able to express it in a more eloquent way, but that's not where my talents lie; I will be the first to admit that my literary skills are not the best. No, what I'm good at is growing things. That's clear in every greenhouse that I have, every plot of tilled earth I own. Time after time my flowers have been the most beautiful, healthiest, and most sought after. Florists from around the world come to buy my stock. They don't blink an eye at the admittedly outrageous prices that I charge. And not only them — major companies, exclusive restaurants, and wealthy private citizens come to my rural part of the world for what I grow.

I've lost count of how many times I've been asked what my secret is, even been offered (discreetly of course) quite large sums of money for my secret "process". It's not really a secret at all. My guiding principle, for all my life, has been that the soil — the foundation — is the most important aspect of growing. With that always in the forefront of my mind, everything that I have turned my rough and calloused hands to has been a wild success.

Well, except for one thing. Her name, her actual name, isn't important. I always called her my Rose. Nothing that I could ever pen could have done justice to who she was. Her head was graced with the warmest, most perfect auburn flow of hair. Her skin was as soft as a spring bud and her eyes were the deepest brown of healthy earth. She was a quiet woman, yet she filled each sentence with the most profound meaning when she chose to speak.

My life had never been happier than when she strolled into it. And for a short, glorious time she seemed to feel the same. I showered her with everything I could: time, trinkets, and, above all, my love. I tried to make more than certain that every moment with me was one that she would treasure as I did. Good soil, see?

Or that's what I thought it to be; it wasn't as good as I had fooled myself into thinking. What I had thought was strong, sturdy growth turned out to only be a healthy-looking façade. For one day, I stopped hearing from my Rose. I called, I searched, and I even tried contacting her friends. It was useless — my oh so lovely flower had decided that she was tired of my careful tending. Several weeks, *weeks* mind you, after our last dinner together I received a letter from her. It dripped with condolences but it was all a flimsy dressing for its true meaning: she had decided that we should not be together any longer.

I brooded, I'll admit it. I was devastated. I could not imagine what else I could have done to cultivate the relationship any differently so that she would have stayed. My life mantra, practically my family's motto, had failed for the first time; I did all to ensure that the soil was rich and nutritious but the crop still failed. I couldn't understand what had happened.

When winter came soon after I had ample time to think in that slow, cold season. The snow that year was vicious. Most of my precious flowers were protected, but even for the ones in the open ground I knew it would be all the better when spring came. The weak would rightfully have the life choked from them and enrich the soil that it had so recently been squandering. Something far better, far more beautiful would arise, fed on the decay.

I suppose that's where the idea came from: Though the plant died, it caused an even greater growth. I concocted a plan to put the only failed effort of mine to a better use; to salvage the best of a terrible situation. This winter I would become the oncoming frost that tore the life away from the dismally performing plant. I know that may sound harsh and terrible but I also know it was necessary. It's just the conditions that are set by nature, and we all have to follow them.

On a moonless night, my crunching footfalls ironically muffled by the hiss of the falling snow, I entered her home. My withered rose was asleep and untroubled. Once she seemed beautiful to me as she slept. Now, though, I found myself revolted.

It took longer than I thought—surely something so diseased shouldn't have taken that long to choke the remaining life from it. But my aching hands and arms afterward were just the first promising results of hard work.

Planting such a cutting was more a labor of patience rather than effort. I kept it hidden away, safe, the chill aiding in the preservation. When the first signs of spring arrived, I knew that the time had come. I dug a shallow hole, for the nutrients should have the shortest possible distance to travel, and on top I planted the seed of a rose. It seemed fitting.

It worked this time as it should have originally. Fed by the soil and maintained thought my attention, the most dazzlingly gorgeous flowers of deepest crimson, almost purple, grew. They were perfumed with the most hypnotizing scent, and the buds were as perfectly full as a nursing mother's bosom. It's the apex of all of my accomplishments, the master craft of my career, made more so for the fact that I had salvaged what I had first thought to be a lost cause. It's the flawless example of what I can achieve and never fails to render awed customers speechless.

Now do you see? There really is no secret. All it takes is good soil.

Carl R. Jennings is by day a thickly Russian accented bartender in Southwestern Virginia. By night he is the rooster themed superhero: the Molotov Cocktail, protecting the weak and beer-sodden. While heroically posing on a rooftop in the moonlight in case a roaming photographer happens by, he finds the time to write down a word or two in the lifelong dream that he can put aside the superhero mantle and utility comb and become a real author. Like Carl R. Jennings' Facebook page or follow him on Twitter @carlrjennings.

Thin Man

Wesley D. Gray

No one believes in the impossible man
the boy has seen outside his dreams
slipping between the clefts of shadow,
a man who slinks through winter nights
and equally lurks in summer days.

A man too slight for this reality,
the Thin Man slides in slivers,
and glides in sways between rays of sun.
He is there awake or dreaming,
and wiggles into waning memories
exuding a miasma of nightmare.

The Thin Man was there
as the boy was plucked
from his home by frozen strangers;
there, when they blackened up his family
with heaps of fresh-turned earth.

And further back,
to the night of bloody wreckage,
within the haze of smoke and fire,
as he watched his mother scream
twisted in heaps of metal,
his father cleaved in glass--
the Thin Man had danced in flame.

And in his dreams
he remembers even more,
but all is forgotten when he wakes.
In these dreams he can see
a crescent grin scraped in rearview,
glinting just before the screech.

Wesley D. Gray is a writer, an author of fiction, and a self-proclaimed poet. His chapbook, Come Fly with Death: Poems Inspired by the Artwork of Zdzislaw Beksinski *is available now. If you're ready to delve deeper, be sure to visit his blog,* Marrowroot.com.

George Talman of Sanford Street

J. R. Restrick

I knocked on the heavy oak door of number 18 Sanford Street, Brooklyn. Waiting in the cold, I admired the workmanship of the majestic Tudor-era portal. It had six panels, elegantly recessed; and intricately carved along the top was what appeared to be a family crest. A distinguished frame gave depth to the entryway. It was an anachronous addition, but had a charming effect, and was not out of spirit with the door itself. Despite the condition of the squalid adjacent homes, I knew I had come to the right place, for I had responded to the tiny advert of one George Talman and his "Shoppe of Antiquarian Curios."

Since the shop was located in the man's attic — and therefore probably his own collection — I couldn't help but wonder if he had been the victim of some misfortune, either failing health or failing finances. As I waited anxiously in the grey morning cold my thoughts were as heavy as my hopes. Visitations were by appointment only. I had telephoned each day for a week to no response. My better senses advised that the proprietor was probably a continent away in search of some marvellous oddity. But why place an advertisement if he did not expect to be in town?

Just as I turned away, I caught movement at the door. A man of unutterably loathsome aspect had at last answered my knock. It was only the motion that arrested my attention, for I heard no creak of hinge, nor any sound of deadbolt nor chain-lock at all.

Taken off guard equally by his sudden appearance as by his disturbing figure, my manners came slowly.

"Uh — Mr. Talman, I presume?" I introduced myself. When he shook my hand, his palm was coarse and his grip awkward. He was a lean, unhealthy man; and though cleanly-shaven he had a filthy look about him. His skin was blotchy from exposure and malnutrition. Overcoming my hesitation, I counted myself in the presence of a devoted adventurer indeed. Yet, his voice was husky, his dialect and language plebeian. Strangest of all, his expensive and quite obviously tailored clothes were several sizes too big.

"Yes?" he enquired, wholly ignorant to the purpose of my visit.

I was temporarily overthrown by the incongruity of his personage. When I recovered I told him I was there about the advertisement.

He looked at me vacantly. "Yes. The *ad-ver-tise-ment.*" He stressed the word slowly, tasting each syllable like a bad whisky.

He opened the door to let me pass. I looked around. The décor reflected a man of distinguished and discerning tastes. I beheld artifacts from myriad dead civilisations estranged one from the other by unconquerable leagues of time and vast expanses of terrestrial space; and somehow, Talman had juxtaposed them in complete harmony via aesthetic principles, such as similarities of design and form.

And yet the floor was littered with garbage. Chief among the lot were high-proof alcohol bottles. The admixture of exotic scents and the unmitigated garbage produced a dreadful smell that flirted grotesquely in the air.

Talman veritably ignored me while I examined the many rarities of his house. "Your home is beautifully furnished, Mr. Talman," I said; "but I perceive these are not the wares you advertised in *The Times.* I am a very serious client, with an eye for the Arabesque. Where, pray tell, is the collection that you advertised?"

"Attic's locked," he said coarsely. "I can't find the key." My host turned away.

Irritated and vexed I was pondering how to proceed when a sudden bell clanged sharply, a single tap, yet the vibrations lingered overlong. I began to feel that I, too, lingered overlong. The sound came from an unlit hallway. I stared into the darkness. From the shadows emerged a cautious creature — a sophisticated Persian cat.

As I am very fond of cats my haste to depart vanished. I went to greet the distinguished pundit. "And just where did you come from, you dashing nabob!" I went to make his acquaintance, and as I did so, I noticed the old cat-ladder positioned within a cubby that appeared to have once held a dumbwaiter.

Discovering that Mr. Talman was a cat enthusiast like me, I put away my escalating repugnance for him. To the very bored-looking man I said, "Mr. Talman, I hate to intrude, but I would quite like to see your collection. Would you mind looking for that key?"

Talman grunted. He looked upon mantels, tabletops, cupboards; he overthrew couch-cushions (pocketing the change therein) and had an altogether aimless aspect as if his search was entirely unguided by any routine of habit or precedence.

Feeling awkward, I turned my attention back to the tawny-coated emir. He squinted unappreciatively as I patted his finely-trimmed pate, but when I satisfied an itch behind the ear he purred affectionately. Now in his confidence, I was free to inspect the red silk collar around the prince's neck. Upon the silver medallion was the gentleman's name: George Talman.

"You named the cat after yourself?" I exclaimed aloud.

"That's right. We call ourselves George," came the answer.

I continued to pat the fond fellow, but as soon as I looked after the progress of Mr. Talman, without warning whatever, neither hiss nor mew, George Talman (the feline) reached viciously at me. I looked back in time to see prehensile fingers spread from the formerly innocuous paws—claws extended! He grabbed my own hand in a ten-fingered vice. Sensible to the trap, I retracted my arm; but his nails were embedded and the wretch pulled me in, biting and clawing! It hissed in glee; and I suffered its breath—oh its foul, fiendish breath!

The cat drew as much blood as it could while escaping retribution. I swiped with my free hand and it scampered off, glaring at me with that haughty Persian air. The devil!

It takes a degree of intelligence to be proud. A creature must be sufficiently aware of its dominance over its surroundings. Such are cats. Maybe I'm personifying the beast more than it deserves, but what can't a proud little creature do once thoroughly content in its own superiority, real or imagined? I refer to the look it gave me before it climbed its ladder. That look: that little I-dare-you-follow attitude! I'm an American of the old stock, but let me say, at risk of sounding too much like our prim cousins. *Well… I… Never!*

"Does that lead to the attic," I asked, pointing upward the fiend's ladder.

"I'm guessing that it does," answered my unapologetic host.

"Do you mind?"

"Please yourself, sir." He found himself, I think, a little too smug in his erudite dwelling, situated no less in such slums of New York as it would have taken a Dickens to describe.

I grabbed the rungs of that old-fashioned ladder and climbed. As I rose I saw two cruel eyes peering from the top, like witch-fire in the darkness. It was young George Talman, fiend of Sanford Street.

That he would have pushed the ladder if he could, I have no doubt. He'd have found another way down, as cats do, and relished among my remains. But he could not. He was poised, I am sure, to claw my face as I emerged. So, I screamed with rage and flailed my mighty Southern arms as I rose. Talman retreated, as do all bullies when one stands up to them. I pulled myself over the top rung into the attic with such a flourish that left no question as to my dominance among the great chain of being, at least as far as the vulgar Mr. George Talman, feline, was concerned! My affectation prevailed. The glinting eyes receded as the cat heeded its better judgement.

And what I saw! The relics—oh the trove of a lifelong antiquarian pursuit! But the most distinctive article in that attic, the thing upon which all my ever-loving sensibilities were fixed toward, was the tattered and defiled form of an aged antiquarian, one Mr George Talman Sr., dead and putrefying upon the floor.

The advertisement concerning antiquarian relics persisted one more week, as per the contracted agreement. Two subsequent newspaper articles followed the incident. The first was a report of the unexpected death of George Talman, aged 58, in his NYC abode on Tuesday November 20, 1923. He had passed away peacefully in his study, coroner's examination testifies. It told also of the unknown squatter found inhabiting Talman's house soon following the tenant's death. That the unidentified homeless man was innocent of murder was evident by post-mortem examination; though residents of the district are advised to vigilantly lock their doors.

The second article concerned the sale of Mr. Talman's effects by government auction in the absence of any legal heirs. The auction is to be held on Thursday, December 13th.

Neither article made any mention of a certain Persian cat, but the surviving George Talman can be spotted occasionally creeping through Sanford Street and into benighted alleys and unknowable foundations. Despite the prizes among the artifacts set for auction, I will not be in attendance. Had Mr. Talman died a natural death, I would not let scruples prevent me from liberating his treasures from less appreciative hands. But if I did engage in the dissemination of his goods, I would be haunted always by an everlasting revulsion. I alone know, contrary to the newspaper reports fabricated in the interest of the sane public, the true nature of Talman's death. The flesh of his neck hanging in ribbons — the gnawed remains of the deceased man's face — the undoubted abject terror on the nascent features. In his final moments, he was conscious of his horrible fate.

For as long as I live, I shall never return to Sanford Street, nor ever again know peace in the company of cats.

J. R Restrick *lives in Maple Ridge, British Columbia. He enjoys wandering the outdoors, where mountain trails, rivers, lakes, waterfalls and the Pacific Ocean are all within reach in one direction or another. He is also fond of fiction from the old pulp days, black and white movies, and strong coffee. His writing has appeared in* The Willows, Weird Tales, Heroic Fantasy Quarterly, *and a forthcoming tale is scheduled to appear in* Nameless Digest

An Existence Photographed

J. J. Steinfeld

In the dead of night of memory
errors and missteps memorized
you look at photographs of your life
none glorious or enviable
some at the edge of nothingness
some in the middle of meaning
some faded others sharp as fear
the light is insubstantial
the selection numerous but incomplete
but you study the miniature biographies
as if they are entrails of eternity
discover hidden in the hideousness
a beauty that mocks beauty
mortality that mocks slow minutes
words cringing at images
images mocking words
the word *mocking* mocking itself.

In the scattering of images
there is a picture of Heaven
slightly torn perhaps tampered with
a dozen or so of Hell
in a strange sort of chronological order

out of spite, you guess,
difficult to rip but easy to misname.

You begin to curse then tumble over your thoughts
the light brightens, it is suddenly morning,
the date uncertain and you smile at a small picture
of yourself smiling in a secret language
the one viewed and the viewer
seeming to know each other
like two lost souls suddenly found.

Canadian fiction writer, poet, and playwright J. J. Steinfeld *lives on Prince Edward Island, where he is patiently waiting for Godot's arrival and a phone call from Kafka. While waiting, he has published seventeen books, including* Disturbing Identities *(Stories, Ekstasis Editions),* Should the Word Hell Be Capitalized? *(Stories, Gaspereau Press),* Would You Hide Me? *(Stories, Gaspereau Press),* Misshapenness *(Poetry, Ekstasis Editions),* Identity Dreams and Memory Sounds *(Poetry, Ekstasis Editions),* Madhouses in Heaven, Castles in Hell *(Stories, Ekstasis Editions), and* An Unauthorized Biography of Being *(110 Short Fictions Hovering Between the Absurd and the Existential, Ekstasis Editions). More than four hundred of his short stories and eight-hundred poems have appeared in anthologies and periodicals internationally, and over fifty of his one-act plays and a handful of full-length plays have been performed in Canada and the United States.*

REPEAT AFTER ME

Matthew J. Hockey

Victoria Harbour – Hong Kong Island – Hong Kong

Shan sucked the final drop of smoke from his vapestick and fought the urge to pitch it off his balcony into the harbour. He'd only been smoking it for a few days since Sujin brought it back from Seoul for him, and he wasn't used to it yet. His monogrammed lighter felt sad and unloved in his pocket and his last emergency Chungwha cigarette rattled around in the carton.

The lightshow boomed and roared from across the water. Even from thirty stories up, he could hear the 'oohs' and 'ahhs' of the tourists gathered on the viewpoints and gangways of the jetty. No matter - the rains would come soon, and that would be the end of all but the most serious travellers. Until the next season at least.

It wasn't cold, but he pulled his mac tighter around himself as he sank into a deck chair. He didn't want to be out here, not while Sujin was inside keeping the bed nice and warm. She didn't want him out there either; she'd made that perfectly clear. They hadn't seen each other for two months while she went back to Korea to visit her family during her university's summer hiatus. Now that she was back they hadn't left the apartment in three days, other than to run down to the atrium and let the Dim Sum delivery man through the security door.

So no, she didn't want him out there. He didn't want to be out there. He had to be. It wasn't a choice. It was business. Sujin had no idea what business he was in. She knew better to argue if he said 'business' in a certain tone of voice. As far as she was concerned he was in import-export.

Yesterday, there was a knock at the door as they lay sprawled the futon. He hadn't buzzed anybody in so he figured it was a neighbour coming to complain about the noise the last two nights. He bundled Sujin away out of sight in the bathroom and went to answer it.

He opened the door half-naked so they'd turn around again without giving him any grief. Except it wasn't a neighbour. It was one of the messenger boys from the pachinko parlour. Lee something something. The kid didn't say anything or even try to look around Shan into the apartment. He passed a note on yellow bond paper, turned on his heel and walked back out.

The note told him to go to a Causeway Bay snake soup place he'd never heard of - not the famous one - and order what the note told him to order. Next day he did, and when the bill came the waiter gave him an antique Nokia flip phone.

"You'll get a call tomorrow at eight. Once you're done destroy the phone."

Eight came, and the lightshow with it. No call. Now the lights dimmed, the music faded, and the tourists spilled back onto the ferries and over to the peninsula for an evening of food and drink. Still no call.

He glanced back to Sujin. She lay sprawled on the bed in a silk gown with cranes flying against a stitched white moon. She stopped reading the Henry James novel she'd been annotating and stared at him over the browned pages. She caught him looking and pushed the gown off one pale shoulder, just enough to make his breath catch in his throat and his hand moved involuntarily for the door handle. She knew he couldn't go back inside, couldn't risk her hearing the call, so she teased him.

She rolled off the bed and came to the door. Shan reached for her; their fingers touched on opposite sides of the glass. *Tell her,* he screamed at himself. Then she stuck her tongue out and twisted the key that locked him on the balcony, and the moment was gone.

"Hey!" He thumped the glass. She ignored him and ducked from view behind his wet bar. Bottles clinked together and she giggled. Not a good sign. Then she burst upwards as if from underwater, Johnny Walker Blue Label held casually by the neck.

"That's not funny. Put it back. I'm serious!" He leant his head on the glass; she cupped her hand around her ear as though she couldn't hear him, then cracked the seal with her thumbnail. She tipped it into a plastic beaker and poured in some cola.

"Are you crazy? You can't. That's... that's sacrilege." The phone rang and he picked it up before the first note had faded. "Shan."

"It's Qiang."

"How did you... how can you... won't the guards be listening?"

"I'm not on the block phones. I've got a private line. There's ways to get anything in Stanley. Though I don't have it for long so I have to be economical. Listen to what I have to say, then say yes or no. Do you understand?"

"Yes."

"Nicolas Fenton, the Brit. He's been working with the OCTB. They caught him doctoring immigration papers for us last year and he's been tipping them ever since."

"How do you—"

"I just know. He knows that I know. He has to go. It has to be you. He won't trust anybody else to get close to him. Double your usual fee. Will you do it?"

Shan pressed the phone against his head until his ear burned.

"Will you—"

"Yes."

The phone died in his hand. He hauled his arm back and threw it out into the harbour. He watched it all the way down, but couldn't hear the splash over the roaring in his head.

Mong Kok – Kowloon – Hong Kong

Shan banged the flat of his hand on the security shutter of a dry-cleaners near the ladies' market. He thought he heard shuffling inside, but couldn't be sure over the racket of a street hawker selling flowers from a pushcart and three people arguing in a tangle of fallen scooters at the corner.

He banged again. The hatch opened in the shutter and a little old lady pulled him inside. She pushed him through the steam and clatter into a forest of plastic-coated dresses that hung down around his shoulders. He found himself in a cramped space filled with boxed powders and chemicals. After a moment, a blind man in a vest and purple shorts pushed inside cane-first.

"Do you have it?" Shan asked.

"Do you?" The blind man held out his hand and clicked his tortoise-shell fingernails together. Shan pressed a bundle of Hong Kong dollars into his hand; he riffled them once and was satisfied.

"How can you tell I haven't given you a stack of Vietnamese Dong?"

The old man's eyes locked onto Shan's face and seemed to squeeze.

"My hands don't lie." He disappeared the money into the back of his shorts and pointed to the front hatch of a broken-down dryer at Shan's knees. "It's in there. QSZ-92 military issue pistol chambered for 5.8×21mm."

"And the suppressor?"

"I machined it myself. Threads straight into the barrel rifling. Measures out at a thirty to thirty-five decibel reduction. Any lower and it would have affected performance. As it stands it's still accurate to thirty metres."

Shan pressed another bundle of notes into the blind man's hands.

"What's this for?"

"Because I like you. Now show me the back way out."

Wan Chai District – Hong Kong Island – Hong Kong

Fenton lived in a concrete and steel apartment complex at the western end of Lockhart Road. Skimpy-clothed Thai and Filipino girls daubed themselves on the front stairs and in the windows of the clubs opposite. There was a time when they had to be paid to do that, a piece of moving eye-candy to bring the customers in. These days they did it all on their own.

Shan drove through a pack of Australians in matching cricket strips to get to the down ramp of a nearby parking structure.

He checked the gun by the light of the dashboard. Once he was sure everything was fine he put it in his right-hand pocket and the suppressor in his left. He walked back to the apartment block.

He slipped inside into a stairwell that smelled of diesel fumes and fresh paint. The elevator worked just fine, but he could see the black plastic bulb of a security camera trained on the door. He took the stairs instead. Fifteen flights, nice and slow so he wasn't breathing heavily at the top.

A strip of plush red carpet ran right to Fenton's door. Everything was edged in gilt; the light fittings, the electrical outlets, the carpet runners and even the stand that held a fire extinguisher.

He put his head to the door and heard the faraway strains of orchestral music. Nothing he recognised. He rang the bell. The music stopped and the door opened on the chain. Fenton's eyes widened with pleasure as he saw who it was. He was a short man for a Brit — fat though, with curly white hair and skin the colour of faded roses.

"My little soldier!" He couldn't get the chain off quick enough. "Come in. Come in. How are you?"

"I'm great. Just had a few drinks down the other end of the road and thought I'd see how you were doing. I wouldn't have bothered you but I heard the music."

"Brahms something-or-other. It's supposed to be calming. Good for the blood. Doctor's orders." He wore a white dressing gown lifted from some long-ago hotel and treated forever after like a family heirloom.

Shan looked around the apartment as Fenton fixed drinks from his cabinet. It was huge for Hong Kong, big enough he had a piano on a specially reinforced section of floor and a chandelier hanging from the ceiling by something no thicker than a ladies necklace. His Burberry coat was wrapped around the top of his hat stand in the corner; a stack of Hong Kong Economic Times lay beneath it.

Shan knew if Fenton turned around and gave him the drink then he'd get talking and he wouldn't do it. He drew the gun and screwed in the suppressor. Fenton stiffened. He must have seen something in the reflection on the bottle. Shan pretended not to notice, to see how the old man would play it.

"You'll forgive me if I withdraw the offer of a drink? I'm not sure I can make a second, my hands have started to shake." He turned around with a pale whiskey clasped in trembling fingers.

"I wouldn't worry about it," Shan said, and Fenton collapsed onto the ottoman.

"How's your mother?"

"Fine. Well, as fine as she gets."

"A real shame that. She always was my favourite, you know... Hold on, I didn't mean that how it sounded."

"I know."

"I liked her."

"I know. She liked you, as far as it goes. Somebody she could talk to, she said. Not like the other girls you had working. She says your name sometimes, when she's up to remembering names. Talks about books she's read and paintings she's seen."

"I have something for her…" He held up his hand for silence when Shan started to speak. "A book. First edition. I know she won't appreciate it. Won't even know what it is, but it will make me happy to know that she has it." He gulped his whiskey, went to the bookshelf, and took down a fat hardback the colour of his skin.

He took three steps towards Shan and opened the book. He dipped his hand inside and came out holding a Soviet-era Tokarev handgun. Shan fired. Once. It punched through the book and blew paste and tattered card all over Fenton's chest. He fell back with one leg on the ottoman and both hands clasped over the hole in his belly, as if he was ashamed of it. His robe fluttered open, exposing an obscene web of varicose veins on his legs. Shan leant close to cover him up.

"Shan Jiawei. Shan Jiawei. Shan Jiawei. Shan Jiawei." It started as a whisper but grew louder and louder. His eyes closed against the pain, sweat beaded on his lips and blood trickled between his knuckles. Still he talked. "Shan Jiawei. Shan Jiawei. Shan Jiawei. Shan Jiawei."

He didn't beg for his mother or mercy or water or God, as so many of those before him had. He just said Shan's name. Over and over and over again. It was weird. Creepy. Perfect diction. Over and over. No mistakes. Over and. Controlled meter. Over. Until finally he took in a breath to speak again and blew it out and was dead.

Shan left.

He made it all the way across town before he realised what had happened. He almost got arrested pulling a U-turn then forced himself to drive the speed limit back to Lockhart Road. He went back inside, breathed the same diesel and paint fumes. Walked the same fifteen flights of stairs and let himself into Fenton's apartment. He was still dead. Still staring at the ceiling with Shan's name on his lips.

"Shan Jiawei. Shan Jiawei. Shan Jiawei!" a voice said in the corner. It sounded so much like Fenton that Shan almost bolted out of the apartment. Instead he moved to the hat stand in the corner and pulled the coat away. It wasn't a hat stand. It was a birdcage lined with newspapers. A huge African Grey eyeballed Shan from its perch.

"Shan Jiawei!" It edged away from him as he aimed his gun. It was an old bird. He remembered it from Fenton's office when his mother went to tell him she was quitting, little Shan clinging to her sleeve.

He opened the cage, grabbed the bird smoothly with its wings held in place so it wouldn't hurt itself. He moved to the window and set it on the ledge. It would probably die. It didn't belong here. But at least this way it would have a chance.

He opened the window. The bird leant out as if testing the air, then flew without looking back.

Matthew J. Hockey *recently returned to Northern England after two years living and teaching elementary English in Seoul, South Korea. His short stories have appeared in* Thuglit, All Due Respect Magazine *and anthologies from* Ghostwoods Books, Falstaff books *and* Crime Syndicate Magazine. *His flash fiction is available online at* Shotgun Honey, Out of the Gutter, Yellow Mama *and* Akashic Books 'Mondays are Murder'.

Lost

Tony Haynes and Ian Stonall

He slid his card into the slot at the automated checkout. The machine addressed him in a civil manner. "If you just bare with me a moment, sir, checking details now."

Max glared at the mechanised till.

"Card number 25471. Mr. Maximillian Scharner. Son of Dieter and Heidi Scharner. Brother of..." The machine seemed to hesitate. "I'm sorry."

"No problem," Max muttered under his breath.

Ignoring the faux pas, the machine perked up again, "I take it I have the pleasure of addressing Mr.. Scharner?"

"No. I broke into Mr. Scharner's apartment this morning and killed him. It was a mercy killing."

An ear-splitting alarm went off and a light above the machine began to flash bright red. Everyone in the store turned to focus on the eye of the storm. Scharner found himself the unwanted centre of attention. A Peace Keeper rushed up to him, relishing the prospect of confrontation. Scharner didn't blame him. A violent interlude was a welcome break from the monotony of existence.

"What seems to be the problem here?" the Keeper asked.

"The gentleman in question is not Mr. Scharner," the machine replied, "but is trying to use Mr. Scharner's card for payment."

The Keeper drew his telescopic night-stick and cracked it open. "If you'd like to step into our back office, sir."

"I was joking."

"What?"

"I am Mr. Scharner. I was attempting a little levity with your checkout assistant here."

"Prove it."

Scharner considered his answer carefully before replying. "No."

The Peace Keeper smiled, then rabbit punched Scharner in the back. He fell to the floor. The Keeper grabbed Scharner's arms, dragged him into the back of the store and began the corrective procedure.

Less than an hour later Max found himself sitting in a small room in the local Peace Bureau. The door opened and a smartly dressed Peace Officer entered. He sat down opposite Max and placed the card that had caused so much trouble on the table.

"I'm free to go?" Max asked.

The Officer nodded.

Max took the card and slipped it into his trouser pocket. The Officer scowled. "Don't you have a wallet?"

"What for? The card is all we have these days."

"Your pocket doesn't seem very safe."

Max stood up. Having noted the location of the camera in the room he leant down with his back to it and whispered to the Officer. "That's the point."

The Officer eyed him coldly. "You realise that I'm duty bound to report your comment."

Max laughed, sarcastically, then left the centre.

Back at his apartment Max played the cat burglar game. Once again, he lost. He was tired of losing. The moment his foot touched the carpet every mechanism in the apartment whirred into life and his Guardian's voice greeted him, "Good evening Maximillian."

Max muttered an expletive under his breath.

"I beg your pardon, I didn't catch that."

"I said fuck off."

"Thank you, sir."

"You're welcome."

"Now what can I get you? A cup of tea? Coffee? Cocoa? Squash? Soda?"

Max knew that if he didn't interrupt his Guardian wouldn't stop until it had listed every beverage known to mankind. "Coffee."

"Black? White? Sugar?"

"Black, no sugar," Max said, though he had no intention of drinking it.

"Right away, sir." A black coffee magically appeared in the food dispenser. The aperture beeped noisily until Max removed the cup. He left it on the kitchen drainer then went and slumped in his favourite battered old armchair.

"Now what would you like to listen to on the radio?" his Guardian asked.

Max closed his eyes. "Nothing."

"Ah, you want to watch television then."

"Not really."

"Shall I switch the Internet on then?"

"No," Max barked.

"But you have to do something."

"I am doing something. I'm trying to relax."

"A little music might help."

"No, it wouldn't."

"You Tube?"

Max buried his head in his hands. If he thought it would have done any good he would have cried. "No," he whispered.

His Guardian momentarily lapsed into silence. "I'm sorry, I don't understand."

"You wouldn't."

"I have to be of use or else my existence is pointless. Please tell me what you want."

"I want to be left alone."

The apartment fell silent. Suspicious, Max peered through a gap in his fingers. Still silence. Had his Guardian finally understood at last? He stood up, closed his eyes, flung his arms out and embraced the beautiful silence.

"Snap, snap, snap, snap, snappy pops. When you feel the urge you gotta pop." The annoying jingle of the TV advert broke the quiet. Naturally it was the ad that Max currently hated the most. As calmly as he could he crossed his apartment, opened his balcony door and stepped outside. Though there was a built-in speaker to the TV on the outside wall at least the volume was marginally lower outside. Or maybe it just didn't sound as loud due to all of the background noise of the traffic. He clasped the railing tightly and stared down at the pavement below. Not for the first time in his life he realised how much he envied his brother, Kurt. Tetchily, he barked out a command. Instantly, the TV switched over to radio. The dramatic, unmistakable sound of Mahler's piano quartet in A minor erupted over the airwaves. Max sighed. He really missed his brother.

Chloe strode purposefully across the room. She had a glow of certainty about her as she approached the desk. The shadowy figure sitting behind the desk bathed in cigarette smoke.

Chloe sniffed the air. Gitannes.

A hand reached up and removed the cigarette from a pair of thin, unsmiling lips. The Senior Peace Officer blew smoke from both nostrils. He reminded Chloe of the dragons she used to feel slightly afraid of in the picture books she used to read as a child.

"Please," the Senior Officer bade her, "take a seat."

Chloe sat down on the rigid uncomfortable chair the other side of the desk. "Thank you."

Ignoring her comment, the Senior Peace Officer glanced down at the file in his hands. "Top of your class in most of the approved subjects. Which did you fail in?"

"I came second in biology and physical education."

"I see." He managed to make the observation sound like a criticism. "It says here that you specifically requested to specialise in social studies. Why?"

"I admire the work you do here. Your aims, your objectives…"

"Flattery will get you nowhere."

"…if I could contribute to them in some small way…" Chloe trailed off in the face of the Senior Peace Officer's cold stare.

"I have a potentially complex assignment that I have just inherited," he said. "I was wondering if you'd be interested."

"I'm honoured that you should consider me, sir."

"I didn't, you were a recommendation," the Senior Peace Officer said. "You certainly have the looks, the question is, do you have the commitment? In all probability, it will most likely turn into a lifetime assignment."

"It sounds intriguing, sir."

The Senior Peace Officer leant forwards and ground his cigarette out in the ash tray on the desk. "Intrigue is something that they write about in novels. Your social skills are supposed to be your great strength, officer Raines, which also means that they are probably your greatest weakness." He handed her the file. "Don't let me down."

Max guarded his corner seat jealously. Though it was impossible to escape from the music, the big screens and the flashing one armed bandits, he tried his damndest. As the cheerful skimpily dressed wait-ress skated past him he held out his glass for a refill. She treated him to one of her standard plastic grins, topped up his glass and then skat-ed away. Max edged back into the booth and attempted to remember a time when he had lusted after such girls.

As the night unfolded he sank into an even greater fit of despair than usual. Gazing around at his fellow patrons, all of whom seemed to be having a fabulous time, he couldn't help wondering if he was the only one who felt so lost, so disillusioned, so alone. Their laughter taunted him. He couldn't work out whether it was genuine or not. De-ciding he needed more vodka he signalled to the waitress again. She hesitated to pour on this occasion. She even stopped chewing her gum. "Haven't you had enough?"

Ignoring the comment Max waved his glass at her. Reluctantly, she poured a single shot. He examined the glass contemptuously. Unsatis-fied with the amount he thrust the glass at her again. "More."

The waitress rolled her eyes and poured until the glass was half full, then retracted the bottle. Max glared at her. "I decide when you stop."

"We're not allowed to serve more than a treble, sir."

Carefully extracting another glass from the dispenser hanging on the back wall of the booth Max replied, "I'll have two trebles then."

The waitress sighed. There really was no hope for some people. She poured him a second drink and then swept away, determined to avoid that side of the bar until he had left. Max was trouble; she could sense it.

Max didn't leave the bar until they threw him out. He sprawled in-elegantly in the gutter and shouted, "See you next week."

Ignoring him, the security staff slammed the doors shut. Max dragged himself to his feet and turned into an alley he knew to be a short cut home. Drunk though he was, half way down the alley, he sensed that he was being followed. The state he was in he realised that there was no way he would be able to outrun whoever it was, so he slouched on the wall and waited for them. When nothing happened, after a few minutes he called out, "What's the matter? You're not usually so shy."

He beckoned the shadows to close in on him. "What are you waiting for? I'm ready."

When still nothing happened, Max wondered if his mind had begun to play tricks on him. Shaking his head, to try and clear it, he set off for home once more. Turning around he walked straight into her arms. With the bravery of drink inside him he hit out, catching her flush on the jaw. She fell backwards and landed awkwardly. Only then did Max realise that he had hit a woman. He knelt at her side and spluttered, "Christ, I'm sorry. Are you alright?"

She reached up and touched his right cheek. Max shrank back from the contact. Chloe smiled at him, then promptly fainted.

⊰✠⊱

Unsure as to what else to do, Max carried her back to his apartment. Desperately he tried to recall the scant bits of first aid he had learnt back when he was at college. His Guardian quizzed him and offered to call the hospital, but Max desisted. The last thing he wanted was any official help. Thankfully, his Guardian had somehow got stuck on the classical radio channel and, at that moment, was playing a soothing Mozart aria from La Nozze Di Figaro. Max lay the bruised girl down on his bed. It suddenly struck him. Ice! That was for a swelling, wasn't it? He hastened across his apartment and requested a few cubes from his dispenser.

"Would you like a drink to go with that, sir?" his Guardian asked.

"No."

"Most unusual."

"What?"

"Nothing."

Once the ice had been dispensed, Max wrapped it in the one clean tea towel that he could find and dashed back into the bedroom. Carefully he applied the improvised ice pack to the girl's head. She opened her eyes and smiled at him. "Thank you."

"You; re welcome."

"You have kind eyes," she observed.

"What?"

"Your eyes, they..." she trailed off as she reached up and touched him.

The gesture made him feel nervous for some reason. He shied away from her hand. "How are you feeling?"

"Not bad considering."

"C'mon then, I'll call you a cab. We'd better get you home. Someone will be worrying about you."

Chloe shook her head.

"Husband? Fiancé? Boyfriend? Family?"

"I live alone."

"Me too." He laughed, but with no feeling.

"What's so funny?"

"It's so easy to think that you're the only one."

"Can I stay then?" she asked.

The idea frightened him. Only then did he feel the true threat that she posed. "No."

"Why not?" she asked, innocently.

"I don't know you."

Chloe beamed at him. She had an alluring smile. Flicking back her fringe she gazed at him intently with her piercing blue eyes. She offered him her hand. "I'm citizen number 25471."

The fear gripped Max's throat. "You can't be." He backed away until he came into contact with the wall. "I'm 25471," he whispered.

Chloe laughed. She had a beautiful laugh. "I'm sorry. It must have been that bump. I meant 741."

"Oh," he said simply.

"Can I ask you a personal question?"

"No."

"Do you believe in love at first sight?"

"Why do you ask?"

"Because I think I love you."

"Don't be ridiculous. You don't even know me."

Chloe looked hurt. "You mean to say, he never mentioned me?"

"Who?"

She reached into her handbag, fished around in it for a few seconds, then withdrew a photograph. She held it up for him to inspect. He couldn't make out the picture clearly from where he stood, so she beckoned him towards her. "I promise I won't bite."

He approached her cautiously. As the picture came into focus he could barely believe his eyes. Forgetting his fear, he snatched it from her hands. The couple in the photograph looked happy and in love.

Kurt looked so young. So did Chloe. Her hair was lighter and her freckles seemed more prevalent.

"He never told me," Max said

"Kurt made me promise to find you if anything ever happened to him. He told me what a sad creature you were. He wanted you to be happy, Max." She hesitated before lowering her voice a notch. "I want you to be happy."

Desire fought his fear. Still he found it difficult to comprehend. "I can't believe he never told me."

"We were only together for a short time."

"When did you meet him?"

"Not long before..." Chloe trailed off.

For the first time since it had happened Max felt his emotions getting the better of him. "I miss him so much."

"Me too."

"I've been looking for you for a long time, Max," she said. "You're not an easy man to find."

"I like it that way."

"Hold me." As he did so he forgot the photograph. It fluttered to the floor. Chloe offered him her lips. "Kiss me."

Max did as he was told.

After carrying Chloe across the threshold of the bridal suite Max kissed her, passionately. He could hardly believe it. It was barely a month since he had first met her. It was amazing how everything suddenly seemed to make sense. The bridal suite's Guardian was playing Mendelssohn's wedding march on a constant loop. He tried to kiss her again. Wriggling out of his grasp, Chloe ducked away from him. He took it as a sign of playfulness and pretended to chase her. She dodged away from him, dodging around the furniture. Max let out an excited laugh. He finally caught up with her by the large glass doors that led outside onto paradise beach. He'd never felt so alive. Pinning her against the glass panel he kissed her neck. Only then did he sense that something was wrong. Pulling away he asked, "What's the matter?"

Chloe shook her head and asked the Guardian to open the doors. The mechanism obeyed and she escaped out onto the beach. Max froze, unsure what to do. His bride turned her back on him and gazed out at the pitiless blue sea. It wasn't until the church service that she had fully realised the magnitude of her assignment. The Senior Peace Officer had texted her his congratulations and informed her that all evidence of her connection with the force would now be erased. Chloe realised that from that moment onwards she was on her own. She tried her best to examine her feelings but she had buried them for so long she struggled to understand them. She felt Max's arms wrap around her waist. She tried to fight back the tears but it was no good. Sensing her pain, he spinned her around. Her tears shocked him and reminded him of the sorrow and frustration that had dominated his own life for years. After a month of bliss, he had almost forgotten. Softly, he asked, "Why are you crying?"

Having had her eyes opened to the true insanity of the world, madness threatened to overwhelm her. She wondered how long she would be able to live with him before killing herself. She choked back the tears and forced a smile to her lips. "Because I'm so happy."

He smiled in response, then sealed her fate with a kiss.

Between them, Ian Stonall *and* Tony Haynes *have sold several short stories to* BBC Radio, Ficta Fabula, Noir Nation, Bete Noir, Daily Science Fiction, White Cat Publications *and* The Big Pulp Magazine.

In addition to this, Tony also writes regularly for Crimson Streets.

www.ingramcontent.com/pod-product-compliance
Lightning Source LLC
Chambersburg PA
CBHW071629140626
46555CB00021B/1689